Whose mouse are you?

ROBERT KRAUS

• pictures by •

JOSE ARUEGO

simon & schuster books for young readers

NEW YORK   LONDON   TORONTO   SYDNEY   SINGAPORE

simon & schuster books for young readers

An imprint of Simon & Schuster Children's Publishing Division

1230 Avenue of the Americas, New York, New York 10020

Revised jacket edition, 2000

Text copyright © 1970 by Robert Kraus

Illustrations copyright © 1970 by Jose Aruego

All rights reserved including the right of reproduction in whole or in part in any form.

SIMON & SCHUSTER BOOKS FOR YOUNG READERS is a trademark of Simon & Schuster.

Manufactured in China

10 9 8

ISBN-13: 978-0-689-84052-4

ISBN-10: 0-689-84052-7

Library of Congress Catalog Card Number : 70-89931

For Bruce and Billy

Whose mouse are you?

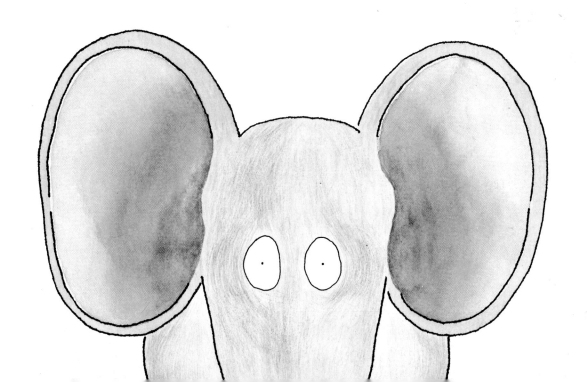

Nobody's mouse.

Where is your mother?

Inside the cat.

Where is your father?

Caught in a trap.

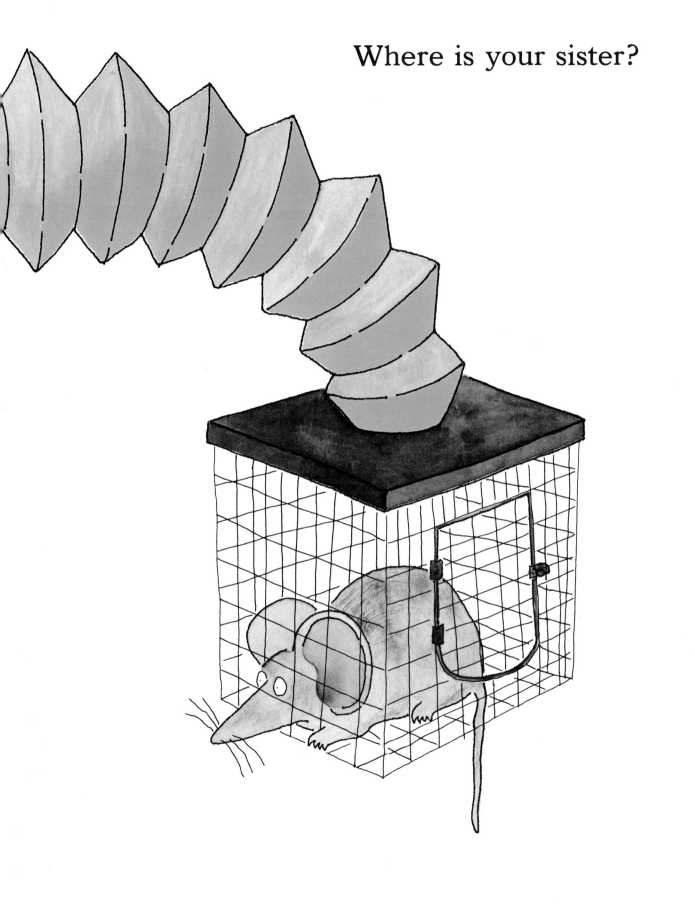

Where is your sister?

Far from home.

Where is your brother?

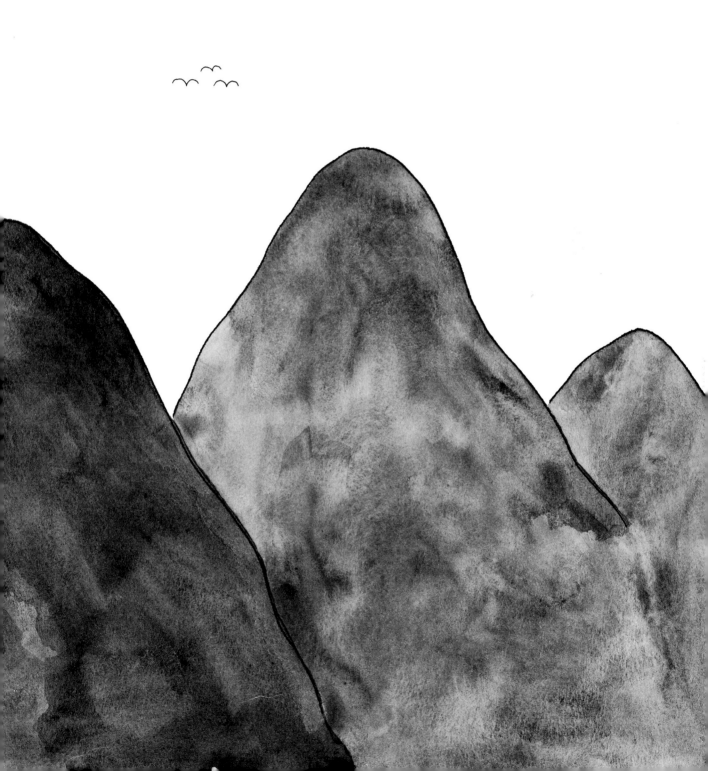

I have none.

What will you do?

Shake my mother out of the cat!

Free my father from the trap!

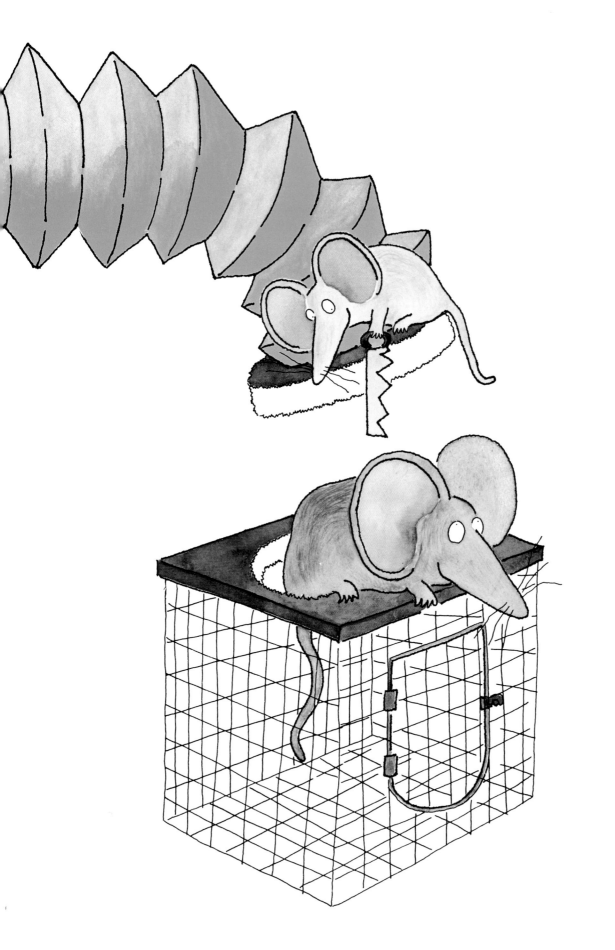

Find my sister and bring her home.

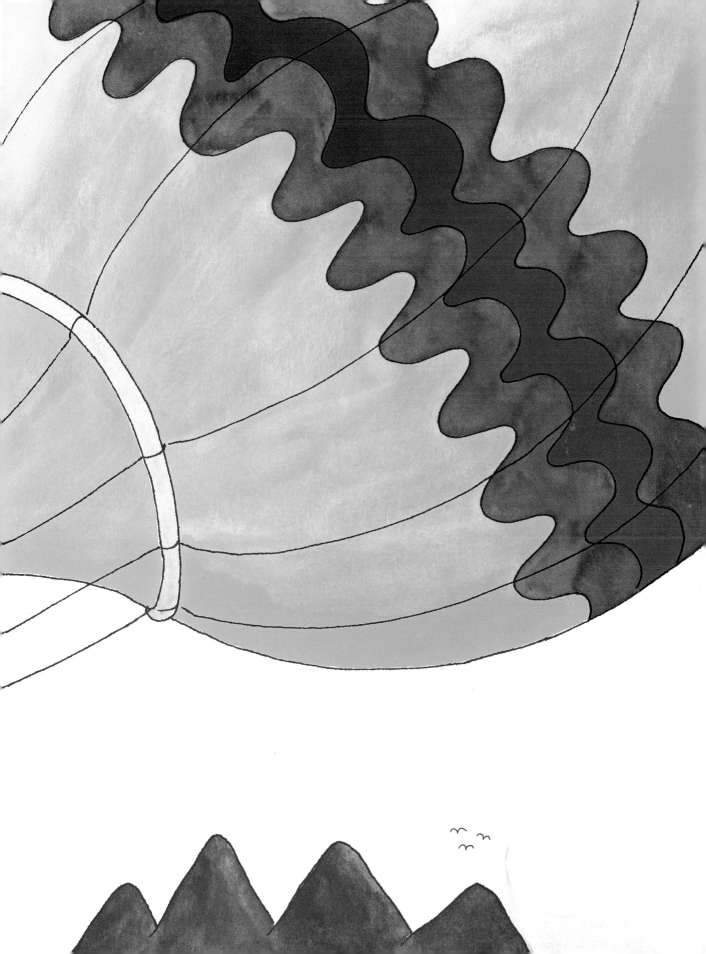

Wish for a brother as I have none.

Now whose mouse are you?

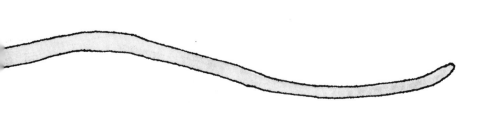

My mother's mouse, she loves me so.

My father's mouse, from head to toe.

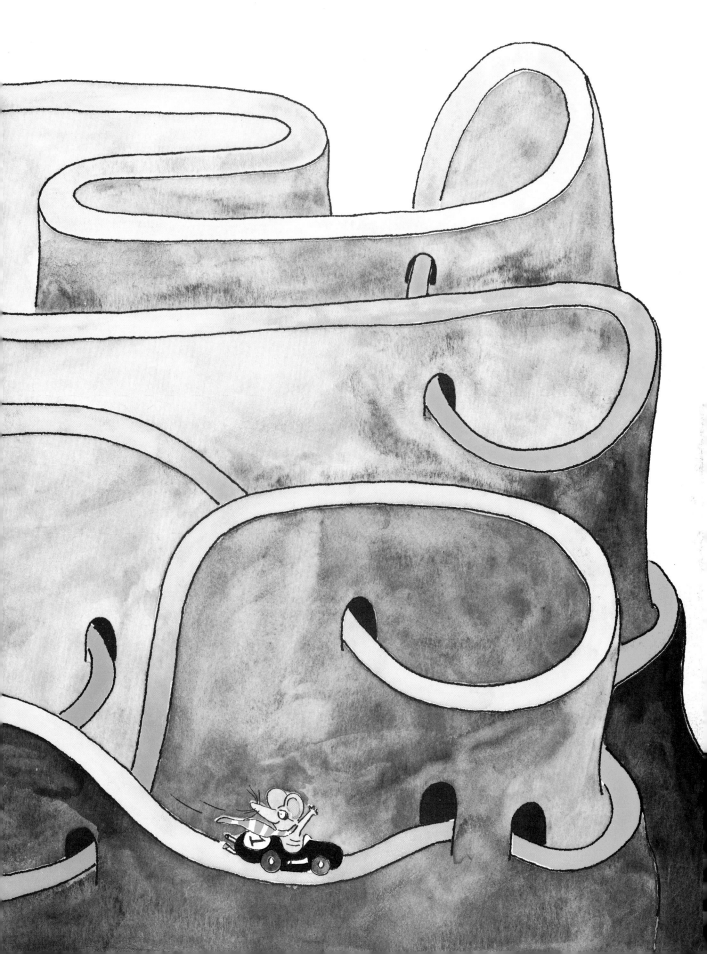

My sister's mouse, she loves me too.

My brother's mouse. . . .

Your brother's mouse?

My brother's mouse—he's *brand* new!